dirty little
TRICK

Dirty Little Trick by Avery James King
Previously published as The Trick by Avery James King

Copyright © 2023 by Avery James King

All rights reserved. No part of this publication may be reproduced, distributed, or transmitted in any form or by any means, including photocopying, recording, or other electronic or mechanical methods without prior written permission of the publisher, except in the case of brief quotations embodied on critical reviews and certain other noncommercial uses permitted by copyright law.

This is a work of fiction. Names, characters, places, brands, media, and incidents are either the product of the author's imagination or are used fictitiously. Any resemblance to actual events, locales, or persons, living or dead, is entirely coincidental. This author acknowledges the trademarked status and trademark owners of various products referenced in this work of fiction, which have been used without permission. The publication and use of these trademarks is not authorized, associated with, or sponsored by the trademark owners.

Editing, Formatting, and Cover Design © Star Child Designs

dirty little
TRICK

TROPES & CONTENT

HALLOWEEN
COLLEGE ROMANCE
INTRUDER VICTIM
BREAK-IN
FRIENDS TO LOVERS
HE FALLS FIRST
DOMINANT / SUBMISSIVE
CHOKING
SPIT PLAY
BREATH PLAY
ANAL PLAY
ORAL
CUM PLAY
SOMNOPHILIA
GRAPHIC SEX SCENES

*For the readers who long to be chased down
by a masked man and made to scream like a good girl.*

CHAPTER 1
RAVEN

Sitting alone in my dimly lit living room, the eerie glow of the TV casts shadows across the walls. The scent of pumpkin spice lingers in the air from the candle in the corner. My attempt to mask the irritation hanging over my head like a gloomy little cloud.

Halloween night, the night I've been anticipating all year long, my favorite holiday of all time, now feels tainted and gross.

I have always loved Halloween. I always found being scared exhilarating. The adrenaline high, your heart racing and senses on overdrive. It's the best thing ever. I am always the first to run into the haunted house. The first in line at the theater when the newest horror film drops.

This is my time to thrive, and it's like the joy of Halloween was sucked right out of the air.

I sigh loudly when the big-breasted blonde on the screen runs upstairs instead of out the front door. Coco looks up at me from her spot beside me, blinking slowly, as if in agreement. I reach out and run my fingers through her soft white fur, happy to have her company tonight.

"At least I know *you'll* never betray me," I say. She meows in response, and I smile.

I never thought I'd be that chick who stays home on Halloween night and talks to her cat, but here I am.

Could I have just sucked it up and gone to the Halloween party at Sigma Nu? Sure. If I wanted to watch my lying, cheating, ex, sucking face with that Beta Kappa Barbie slut.

Hard pass.

Admittedly, it killed me a little bit to have to miss it.

Skylar and I were together for a year, and then I learn through the campus blog that he was caught — by her boyfriend, no less — bending the little Kappa Queen over a shelf in the stacks.

The nerve of some people, I swear.

Apparently, they've been screwing in secret since the summer. I say good riddance, let her have him.

My best friend, Griffin, on the other hand? He says Sky needs to pay.

Griff was never really a big fan of Sky's. He never thought Sky was good enough for me, and I thought at one point that maybe he was just feeling a little jealous or left out. We used to spend all of our time together, and then suddenly my attention was split between him and another guy.

Sky was under the impression that Griff was jealous for other reasons. Namely, that he wanted me for himself, but I assured Sky that wasn't the case. Griff and I may be extremely close, but he's never felt that way about me.

Griff could have any girl he wanted, and there are definitely plenty of them that want him. Who could blame them? With his dark disheveled hair hanging down in those metallic gray eyes. Sometimes it was like he could stare straight into my soul. His broad shoulders, fit body, and angular features leave the sorority girls drooling, but they never seem to do it for him.

When he found out about Sky and Kiersten, the Kappa Slut Supreme, his first reaction had been one of disgust.

"Are you fucking joking? Her?"

His second reaction…?

"I'm gonna kill him."

I instantly declared a no-maiming order, and Griff said he'd play nice, but the glint in his eye said otherwise.

"He can't just get away with this shit, Rave. You've been nothing but good to him, and then he turns around and fucks Keirsten Post?" he scoffs, shaking his head in disgust. "He can't get away with this."

I chuckle, leaning my head on Griff's shoulder. "As much as I agree, I don't want to make a big deal out of it. He's an ass, and I'm done with him."

Griff sighs derisively, kissing the top of my head. "Fine."

Did I honestly believe that meant Griff didn't have something planned? No, not really. But hey, I tried.

I'm over it. Honestly, I haven't even cried. He's not worth the tears, but that doesn't mean I haven't bottled it all up and let it fester this last week.

My phone vibrates beside me on the couch, and Coco meows in protest.

I reach for the remote and pause the movie right as the killer readies to stab the female lead, his knife halted in mid-air.

Kelsey's name flashes across the screen, and I swipe to answer.

"Hey," I answer, the chaotic sounds of the party echoing in the background.

"Girl, you are not going to believe what just happened!" she shouts. I can picture her on the edge of the room, one hand pressed to her ear as she holds her cell to the other.

"Kelse, I don't want to know what stupid shit Sky did. We aren't together anym—"

"Raven, the lacrosse team just stormed in here and beat the shit out of him," she says, laughing in shock.

I sit up straight, dropping my feet to the ground. Griffin is the captain of the lacrosse team. If he told them to, they would all follow his lead and deliver the beating he thought Sky deserved.

"Is Griff there?" I ask.

"I don't know. I didn't see him specifically, but it was definitely his team. I never forget an ass," she says.

"Stop checking them out and find out where Griff is, please," I sigh, and she laughs.

"Hold on," she says.

Switching to speakerphone, I pull up my contacts and send a quick message to Griff while Kelsey searches for him.

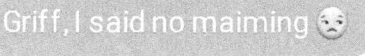

Three dots dance across the bottom of the conversation, and I know he's responding.

Guess

I huff, leaning back into the cushions, typing out a reply.

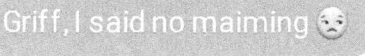

I smirk, staring down at his message.

"I don't see him anywhere," Kelsey's voice shouts, filling the room.

"It's okay, girl. I texted him," I say.

"He has it so bad for you," she giggles, sounding on the verge of drunkenness.

I roll my eyes and stand from the couch.

"No, he doesn't. It's called being a good friend," I say.

"You keep telling yourself that, Rae. But when he gets

in your panties, remember I called it. And I want *all* of the dirty details," she laughs.

"Oh yeah? And what makes you think there will be any dirty details?" I chuckle, making my way around the couch toward the kitchen for a snack.

I should be more annoyed, but honestly, I'm not. I only wish I could have seen it with my own eyes. I'm sure there will be plenty of videos circulating tomorrow.

"Umm, have you seen your best friend before? That man was built to fuck. I'm honestly a little jealous that you're gonna be the one to sample the goods," she says. Okay, maybe borderline drunk was being generous.

"Okay, sounds like you need to lay off the booze and drink some water," I say.

"Yes, Mommy," she teases.

"Be good, and stay safe," I tell her.

"Will do, love you, Rae."

"Love you, too, Kelse," I say, dropping my phone on the island before opening the refrigerator door.

"Coco, remind me to go shopping tomorrow," I say, when I don't find anything appealing.

She meows in response, and I reach out to scratch her beneath the chin. "Thanks, pretty girl. Should we check the cabinets?"

A loud crash sounds from the backyard, and Coco leaps down from the counter. Her startled yowling makes me jump, and I clutch my chest.

"What the hell was that?"

Leaning up onto my tiptoes, I stretch out over the kitchen sink to peer through the window. I can't really see much; the interior lights reflect too brightly for me to make anything out.

Coco races toward the back door to investigate, but I don't want her going out and getting hurt.

"Coco, no." I chase down the hallway after her, but she slips through the cat door before I can grab her.

"Shit," I hiss under my breath.

My heart beats wildly in my chest. What if there's someone out there? I mean, I live in the middle of a college town. With it being Halloween, everyone is out. Who knows what the hell made that sound.

It very well might have just been a neighborhood dog, but if that's the case, I really don't want Coco out there.

I reach for the handle and turn the lock before I pull the door open slowly, just enough to peer out through the gap.

And that's when I see what made all the noise.

"What the fuck?"

AVERY JAMES KING

CHAPTER 2
RAVEN

The night is dark, despite the crescent moon overhead, shining faintly through the swaying branches of the tall oak trees, and what I can make out is absolute chaos.

My trash cans are knocked on their sides, contents scattered like confetti in the wind.

I step out slowly onto the back step, gripping the doorknob tightly in my hand in case whatever knocked them over is still out here.

The wind picks up slightly, lifting a paper napkin from the mess and dancing it across the yard until it disappears into the shadows beyond my fence.

A chill races up my spine, and I wrap my arm around my middle to keep from shivering. It isn't particularly cold, but I don't want to stand out here any longer than necessary.

Reaching back inside the doorway, I fumble for the light switch, but when I flip it on, nothing happens.

"Are you shitting me?" I curse, wide eyed.

I step back in, staring at the stupid switch as if I can scare it into submission. I flip it on and off aggressively, but the damn thing doesn't light.

"Of course," I huff, stepping back out onto the steps.

Maybe she just needed to use the little kitty's room. Not like she doesn't have a perfectly good litter box inside, but what do I know?

"Coco," I hiss into the night, kissing into the velvety darkness when she still hasn't come back.

I stare hard into the shadows, but can't seem to focus my eyes well enough to make anything out. I stamp in frustration. She's solid white, for goodness' sake; she shouldn't be that hard to find.

"Coco, girl, come on," I try again, snapping my fingers a few times before I pause to listen.

It's no use though. I can't hear anything over the rushing sound of my heart beating out of my chest.

Chewing on the inside of my cheek, I consider turning around and going back for my phone. If I had a light, it would make things a lot easier.

Until you catch a pair of glowing eyes watching you from the bushes.

The thought makes me shake and shuffle my feet backward a half step.

"Come on, Raven," I mutter to myself, "pull yourself together. It's just because of the movie. Nothing is in the bushes."

Drawing in a steadying breath, I release the doorknob

and step to the edge of the concrete steps, leaning forward to peer across the yard.

Nothing.

Coco is nowhere to be seen, and I'm starting to get worried.

"Damn it, Coco. If you die out here, I'm going to be so mad at you," I hiss, tears pricking the corners of my eyes.

Another tentative step forward, and I descend the stairs until I reach the last one, toes on the very edge of the concrete, tickled by the dew-covered grass.

"Shit," I whisper, not wanting to walk across the wet grass with my bare feet.

"Coco… here kitty-kitty," I sing out to her in a shaky voice.

The tree limbs sway in the breeze, rustling the leaves and lend to the eerie quality of the moment. But when the breeze dies down, and the rustling continues, I squeeze my hands into fists at my sides until the biting of my nails against my palms is all I can feel.

"Come on, Coco, this isn't funny," I call through clenched teeth, my fear growing with every passing moment.

The sounds abruptly stop, and I freeze.

Drawing in a shaky breath, I stare into the shadows and take a step forward, willing my cat to come to me. The cool blades lick at the bottom of my feet until I reach the middle of the yard.

What if she was hurt? What if whatever knocked over the trash cans had grabbed her?

"Coco," I squeak out, voice cracking in fear.

The darkness presses in all around me, and all I can think of is to run. Run back inside, call Griff, and have him come over immediately to help me find her.

But what if Coco can't wait that long? I have to find her now.

I draw in a breath and hold it tight until my lungs are burning. Counting down in my head, I ready myself to march the rest of the way across the lawn to investigate. But before I can even lift my foot, the bushes stir again.

Breath caught in my throat, my eyes brim with tears.

"Please," I whisper, clutching my fists in fear.

With my mind running wild, images of shadowy figures and rabid beasts fill my mind, and a cold sweat breaks out across my brow.

And then, a flash of movement and a loud yowl send me reeling backward.

Coco leaps from the shadows, tail flicking back and forth in annoyance. Her pretty little head tilts when she sees me standing there in the darkness, clutching my chest in terror.

"Fuck, Coco… that wasn't funny," I scold her, but she doesn't seem to care that she very nearly sent me to an early grave.

She prances past me and bounces up the stairs, disappearing inside like nothing happened.

"Damn cat, I nearly pissed my pants," I call toward her, dropping my hands back to my sides.

I turn and glance back over my shoulder at the scattered trash. It's going to have to wait until daylight. I'm not standing out here in the dark for another second.

Trekking back through the wet grass, I ascend the stairs and walk inside, closing the door behind me.

Coco dances between my wet feet, rubbing herself against my legs as if in apology, but I'm not buying it.

"Yeah, have fun out there, did you?" I say, annoyed and ready to dry my feet off.

I bend down to pet her, and the little brat dodges my hand, bolting for the cat door again.

"Oh, no you don't," I yell and grab her around the waist before her back half makes it through.

I pull her back in and hold her to my chest as I lock her little door for the night.

"No more late-night adventures for you, bitch," I say, and she whines up at me.

"I know, I'm horrible. Deal with it," I say, dropping her to the ground and watching her scamper back to the couch.

Just as I'm about to follow her, I have the urge to peek out the window one last time, just to be sure nothing is out there. With the yard still empty, I drop the curtain and reach for the lock, twisting it into place.

Just to be safe.

AVERY JAMES KING

CHAPTER 3
RAVEN

Walking back into the kitchen, I lean forward, resting my elbows on the counter and cradling my head in my hands. My heart is gradually returning to its usual steady beat.

Being out there in the dark, all of my senses practically cut off, was suffocating. Being back in my warm, dimly lit living room, washes of warm buttery light flickering against the wall behind the candle, I feel like I can finally take a breath. Like the weight of the shadows closing in around me has lifted.

"Let's never do that again. Alright?" I say, lifting my head to peer over at Coco. She sits perched on the arm of the couch, watching me with her cool, unaffected gaze, completely unbothered.

Drawing in a deep breath, I push myself up off the counter and smooth down my shirt.

"Okay, snacks. I need snacks," I announce, back to exploring the contents of my cabinets.

They're pretty barren right now. I've been distracted ever since the breakup and take out has become my go to. I need to plan a trip into town tomorrow to replenish my stock. I may even score some half-price Halloween candy, and there is nothing wrong with that.

When I come across one lone bag of popcorn, I feel like I've hit the jackpot. Perfect for my scary movie night.

I pop the bag into the microwave and hit start.

"Alright, I'm going to go pee really fast. You watch the popcorn," I tell Coco as I run upstairs.

I can just make out the faint sound of popping once I've finished and exit my en suite bathroom. A chill skates across my arms, probably an aftereffect of adrenaline. I catch sight of Griff's lacrosse hoodie hanging over my corner chair and reach for it. He's always forgetting stuff like this over here, but I don't mind. I usually just end up stealing it from him, anyway.

The thought gives me pause. Could he be doing that on purpose, knowing that I'd more than likely end up wearing it around campus? I know anytime I did, Sky would get really moody and complain that I never wore his clothes around campus. Forget that his Greek letters were all over his clothes, and wearing someone else's letters was a big no-no as far as traditions went.

Shrugging, I pull the hoodie down over my head and lift the collar to my nose, drawing in the spicey scent of Griff's cologne.

He always smells so good. Letting my mind wander, I

walk back downstairs.

Say Griff *was* leaving me with his clothes on purpose. Say Kelsey wasn't wrong, and Griff really did have a thing for me. Why wouldn't he have ever said anything? Sure, we've always been close, but is it possible that he's been sitting on the sidelines all this time, waiting for me to notice him?

Better question: could I even go there with Griffin?

Kelsey's comments from earlier comes to mind, and the image of Griff's naked body infiltrates my thoughts. I've never actually seen him naked, just in his boxer briefs, but it isn't hard to imagine what he's got underneath them.

When I get back downstairs, the movie is already playing.

I furrow my brow, knowing that it was still paused before I went upstairs. But when I approach the couch, Coco is sprawled out on her back, the remote tucked beneath her.

"Really? You couldn't wait two minutes?" I say to her, pulling the remote out and pausing the movie once more, and setting the remote on the coffee table before heading into the kitchen.

I replay my conversation with Kelsey again, my mind wandering back to Griffin.

When he gets in your panties, remember I called it.

I picture his hand slipping beneath the waistband of my jeans, beneath the hem of my panties. His fingertips calloused from years of playing lacrosse. Would he take his time, drawing out every movement? Or would he waste no time making me fall apart beneath him?

Skylar was never the type to take his time. He acted like if we didn't have sex in record time, he would miss out on getting off. Like it was some prize for winning a race.

I bet Griffin would take his time. Touch every inch of me, savor every taste. Lick every—

The microwave beeps loudly, drawing me back to the present. My cheeks are flushed and warm, and I press the backs of my cool fingers to them to cool myself down.

I pull the popcorn from the microwave and set it on the counter in front of me.

Griff and I met in psychology, freshman year. He sat behind me and had forgotten his laptop in his dorm room, leaving him unable to take any notes.

I remember him sitting there quietly, listening to the best of his ability, but Professor Roth went heavy on the introduction notes that day. When he'd sworn under his breath, I turned and noticed him holding a pencil in his fist, lead broken. I'd offered him a consoling smile before reaching into my bag and pulling out an ink pen and handing it back to him.

His thankful expression made me smile. I remember thinking he was cute.

When the class had ended, he tried returning my pen.

"Keep it," I told him.

"Thanks," he said, standing and tucking it into his front

pocket. "I'm Griffin, by the way."

"Raven," I smiled before drawing my lower lip between my teeth and packing my laptop into my bag.

He'd just continued to watch me, the corners of his lip twitching like he was holding back a grin. His dark eyes took me in, and I felt exposed.

"I, uh... recorded the lecture to go over later tonight. I could send you the audio clip if you wanted," I offered, watching his eyes light up.

"That would be amazing," he'd said.

He gave me his email, and I sent the files over that night. The next day, he'd waltzed into class and sat down right beside me. He's been by my side every day since.

Even after Skylar and I started dating. If he liked me, wouldn't he have backed away after that?

Searching the cabinets for a bowl, I think about how he'd clearly disliked the idea of me and Skylar. He'd made fun and teased me about him for weeks in the beginning. But after a while, he stopped.

He's never been a fan, but it was like he tolerated him for my sake.

But what if he was just biding his time?

I stand there, contemplating, and pull the collar of his hoodie up to my nose again. His dark, bottomless eyes flash in my mind as I inhale, and my stomach flutters.

Fuck... those eyes, staring into mine with his smell all around me, and his body... damn, he really does have a nice body.

Grabbing a bowl, I make up my mind. I'm going to text him. See if he wants to come over and watch a movie with me. Gauge the situation with new eyes.

Feeling those butterflies again for the first time in ages, I laugh to myself, pulling open the bag of popcorn and dumping it in the bowl.

CLICK.

The sound of a door snicking shut freezes me in place. My eyes go wide and my heart hammers in my chest until it drowns out everything around me.

CHAPTER 4

RAVEN

My feet refuse to move, frozen in place as the silence rings in my ears.

I know what I heard, and I know that I locked my doors, so what the fuck was that sound?

I cut my eyes to Coco, who doesn't seem to notice the panic rolling off me in waves. She's still laying in her spot on the couch, oblivious to my terror.

But if there was someone in my house, she would know. She'd prance over and investigate, like before. Right?

Suddenly, I want Griff here for a whole other reason.

Tiptoeing across the room, I go to grab for my phone… but it's gone. I frantically scan the area, lifting up pillows and moving Coco aside, much to her annoyance, but my phone isn't here.

I didn't take it with me upstairs. I left it here.

Or… maybe I set it in the kitchen and just overlooked it?

Turning back to the kitchen, I scan the counters and come up empty.

Tears prick my eyes, and my hands shake violently. I know that I had it before going outside. I'd texted Griff and set it down before looking for a snack. And then the trash cans toppled over outside and… I stood out back, searching for Coco.

I couldn't have been out there for more than two or three minutes, tops. But…

I turn and take in the front door. It's unlocked.

My throat constricts with fear and my mouth falls open, panic and confusion washing over me.

I locked that door when I got in tonight. It's a habit, living here alone. I always make sure it's locked. But especially tonight, on Halloween, when the whole town is out getting drunk and going crazy. I didn't want anyone accidentally stumbling inside drunk, searching for a place to crash. Or worse, Skylar thinking it would be a good time to crawl back and convince me I was overreacting.

No, that door was locked.

And now it's not.

Pins prick at the nape of my neck, anxiety coiling in the small of my back, ready to spring at a moment's notice.

My chest heaves with each shaky breath I draw in, and it's enough that now Coco is sitting up and watching me, concern clear on her fuzzy little face.

Wracking my brain, I run options through my mind.

I could grab Coco and run out the front like any logical person would. But what if I open the door and there's someone waiting on the other side, ready to snatch me up?

I could run back into the kitchen and arm myself with a knife. Not that I have one anywhere big enough to do real damage to someone.

I have pepper spray and a rape whistle in my bag upstairs... and my laptop. I could run upstairs and FaceTime Griff and then hide in my closet until he showed up.

Just then, Coco draws back, yowling low and mean. A clear warning.

Spinning around, I follow her gaze, looking down the hallway toward the back door... standing wide open. The curtains blowing in the breeze.

Tears spill from my unblinking eyes as I watch in horror as it swings slowly shut. As if guided by a gentle push.

"H-h-hello?" I stutter as I try to call out.

I sidestep toward the couch, ready to grab Coco and run, when the lights go out through the entire house.

I scream before reaching up and covering my mouth with trembling hands. Forcing back a sob, I hunch down until I'm tucked behind the far side of the couch.

THUMP, THUMP, THUMP.

Slow and steady steps echo through the silence.

Heavy booted feet. An unmistakable intruder. And then a shadow, sliding across the floor, until finally a large, hooded figure stands at the end of the hallway. He's blocking the back door and has a clear view of the front.

I'm trapped. Like one of those stupid girls in the movies. How am I supposed to get out alive? His large frame is no match for me. He'd toss me around without any hesitation.

Sinking to my hands and knees, I crawl along the front of the couch, doing my best to stay out of sight. When he starts to approach, I get this adrenaline filled urge to bolt for the stairs.

Coco hisses loudly before leaping away and disappearing into the shadows. I can't blame her for leaving me this time.

When the intruder steps into the room, he stops. His head turns from side to side, surveilling the room, looking for me.

I do my best to quiet the hiccupping sobs threatening to rip free of my chest, but it's no use. The muffled whimpers catch his attention, and I see it when he finds me.

His head tips to one side, and even though his face is completely hidden from view, I have the eeriest feeling that he's grinning at me.

"Run, little Raven. I've been dying to catch you," his low voice skates over my skin, like static electricity.

He takes another step toward me, and I leap forward.

Every ounce of self-preservation kicks in, and I cry out, stumbling for the stairs. I don't look back to see if he's following me. I don't stop to try to divert him.

I just run.

CHAPTER 5
RAVEN

The intruder's footsteps echo menacingly behind me as I race for the stairs, the bubble of fear bursting from my chest, ripping free in a terrifying scream. I grab onto the banister and pull myself forward, each step creaking beneath the weight of my desperate sprint.

I was going to die tonight. I was going to be killed, and I didn't know why. Was this just some coincidence? The man behind me only targeting me because he somehow knew I was home alone. Or did he perhaps know me? Was there a reason he was coming after me?

As my feet scrambled up each carpeted step, I couldn't help the thoughts circulating in my mind.

I'd never been outright mean to anyone, always easy to get along with. So I couldn't fathom someone having a vendetta against me, or a reason to target me.

Aside from Kiersten, I never had an issue with anyone on campus, and *she* cheated with *my* boyfriend. I'm the one who should have a score to settle here.

I hear it the very second his boot comes into contact with the bottom stair, and I push myself to run a little faster. But my feet don't react as quickly as my brain, and I slip, sliding backward a few steps.

"Be careful, little Raven. I'm right behind you," his low voice calls out from behind me, and I cry out in fear.

The backs of my knees tingle as my fear reaches a tipping point. My legs nearly give out again, knowing he's right behind me. It's as if I've touched a live wire, my body ready to burst.

The dim light of the moon filters in through the curtains, casting eerie shadows on the walls. The sight of my usual safe haven now seems distorted, and almost nightmarish. The stairs stretch out endlessly before me.

His footsteps draw nearer, and I feel his fingertips graze the hem of my top, just missing me.

I pitch forward, clambering up the final steps and race down the hallway toward my room.

Once I'm inside, I spin around and see him approaching. He's less than five steps from my door, and I grab it quickly, shoving it closed, putting all of my weight behind it.

I reach down and spin the lock into place, shuddering as I take a tentative step backward.

BOOM!

He hits the door and I curl in on myself, shaking violently as the absolute worst fills my mind. I see my laptop in the corner and race toward it. When I lift the face open, I'm relieved to see it still has power. But when I attempt to Facetime Griff, the call doesn't connect.

No service.

I curse myself, turning away from the glowing screen as another blow shakes the door.

"Come on, little Raven. Open up and let me inside," his voice beckons.

I pause, the timber of his voice stroking the edges of my mind. A familiar tug that tells me I know that voice, but fear clouds my ability to think clearly.

Another fist to the door, and the curiosity is gone. I turn to search for my pepper spray when a loud thump and crash explode behind me.

I whirl around just in time to see my door fly open, splinters of wood spraying the floor, and the hooded figure standing there looking right at me.

"No!" I scream and turn, but I'm not fast enough.

His arms circle around my waist, lifting me up against his chest, and I am immediately surrounded by the heat radiating off his body.

"Let me go!" I yell and thrash wildly.

"Calm down, little Raven," he says into my ear, and I still.

That scent. I know that scent.

Spicy and warm, like the hoodie I'm wearing.

Suddenly the low voice rumbling in my ears breaks through the terror and I spin my head to the side.

His face is shadowed, but I can just make out the grin spreading across his face.

"What the...?"

Before I can say another word, he spins and tosses me onto my bed, crawling over me until his face hovers just inches from mine.

"What's the matter, little Raven? Aren't you happy to see me?" he asks, smiling down at me with a devious look in his eyes.

"Griff?"

CHAPTER 6
GRIFFIN

I take in her wide-eyed, shocked expression and smile down at her. Her chest rises and falls in quick succession, and her eyes are still wet with tears.

"You absolute shit," she swats at my chest and I grab her hand, pinning it over her head.

She lets me, too.

The number of times I've pictured her in this position beneath me is more than I can count. Until today, I've always maintained a safe distance, waiting for that dumbass, Skylar, to fuck up. I always knew he would, too. I just never expected to want to kick his ass as much as I do for it.

But Raven asked me not to, so I didn't. Not personally, anyway. I just got my team to dole out the beating for me.

I never promised he wouldn't get one. Just that I wouldn't do it personally. Though, I'm still having second thoughts about it.

"Scare you?" I ask, voice still low and scratchy.

"Umm, yes!" she exclaims sarcastically.

I knew it would. But I also know how much she loves being scared, so I wasn't really worried about causing any real damage. She gets off on this shit, and if I'm being totally honest, I did, too.

There was something so primal about the whole thing. After accidentally knocking over her trash — which clearly worked to my advantage — I watched her chase Coco outside. I took the opportunity to run around front and swipe her phone before heading back to watch her from the bushes.

Coco's little ass almost blew my cover, too. She wouldn't leave my side, and I knew I would get caught if I didn't act fast. So, I scooped her up and rubbed her on the tummy, where it irritated her the most. She hissed at me and jumped free, scaring the crap out of Rave in the process.

I knew her emotions would be on high alert after that.

"You know you loved it," I say, touching the end of my nose to hers playfully.

"How the hell did you get in here? I locked the doors," she asks, laying there beneath me, in no rush to pull away.

Hmm... interesting.

Curiosity piqued, I drop down onto my left forearm and shift my weight to one side. The left side of my body brushes hers as I reach down into my pocket and pull out a set of keys. I notice her body go still for just a moment, her throat bobbing as she swallows hard.

I dangle the keys in front of her face, and her face falls in annoyance.

"Fuck, I didn't even think of that," she says, rolling her eyes.

"You weren't supposed to," I laugh, returning the keys to my pocket.

I roll back to center, practically laying on top of her. She watches my expression, and I want so badly to lean down and press my lips to hers, but I don't.

Her eyes suddenly go wide, and I pull my head back a fraction.

"You broke my door," she says accusingly.

"I'll fix it," I tell her, chuckling over her shocked expression.

"Not the point, Griff."

"Well, you locked me out, and I was *very* motivated to get inside," I say, dropping my voice low again and trailing my eyes over her throat. I can just make out her rapid pulse fluttering beneath her jaw.

"Oh, were you?" she says, arching her eyebrow as she looks up at me.

"Yeah," I respond, sinking lower.

Her hips shift and she parts her legs, drawing her knees up on either side of my waist. I've already adjusted to being in the dark, and I can just make out the glint in her eyes.

"I didn't like the idea of you missing out on your favorite holiday because of that dumbfuck," I say, releasing her hands and trailing my fingertips down her arm and over her shoulder until my hand is resting at the base of her throat. "You love being scared, and I wanted to scare you. Get you out of your head and make your heart race."

I slide my hand higher until I can feel her pulse points beneath my fingers. Her heart is hammering, and she is breathing more heavily now. "Mission accomplished," I whisper into the space between us.

Drawing my bottom lip between my teeth as I think about tightening my grip on her pretty little throat. Just enough to make her head swim.

She raises her chin slightly, and when I lift my eyes to hers, there's a challenge there.

"Do it," she whispers, as if she read my mind.

Hell, she probably did. We get each other like that. She's always been in sync with me, and that's why it killed me when she and Skylar started dating. I knew he would do something to fuck everything up, but I didn't expect it to take two years.

"Rave," I warn her.

I only have so much strength, and I've done my best to fight my urges these last few years. But if I start, I won't be able to stop. Ever.

"You know you want to," she tempts me.

"I don't want to do anything unless you're actually over him," I tell her. There is no way I'm going to be able to handle it if she changes her mind and goes back to him. I can't have her regretting anything that might happen between us.

"I am," she says and raises her hips to meet mine, brushing against my hard cock. "And now I'm under you. So do something."

"Fuck," I hiss at the contact, rolling my eyes back and squeezing them shut.

"Griff," she says, like a whispered plea, and I lose all control.

I tighten my fist around her throat and grind my hips down between her spread legs. Lifting her by the throat, I draw her mouth to mine, hovering over her parted lips.

I don't kiss her. Not yet. I just barely graze my lips over hers before flicking my tongue out and licking at her upper lip.

A moan catches in her throat, and I grind into her again, watching her eyes flutter closed.

Then I release her.

Her breaths come heavy and fast, and I'm obsessed.

Using my thumb, I lift her chin until her head is angled back, and I lean down to drag the tip of my nose against her throat. She smells like a mixture of the both of us. Toasted marshmallows and earthy spices. It's intoxicating.

Her hands find the bottom of my jacket and slip

underneath, smoothing over my stomach and sending a shiver through me.

"If you want me to stop, now would be the time to tell me," I say, possessively biting down on her throat. It isn't enough to leave a mark... yet.

"I don't," she says, panting.

Her fingers dip inside the waist of my jeans and tug me closer.

"Tell me this isn't going to ruin our friendship," I say, and pray that this isn't a heat of the moment's decision on her part. I've wanted this for years, and I know that this is new for her. If that means I have to get up and walk back downstairs right now, I will.

"It won't," she assures me, but I'm not completely sold.

"How can you be sure?" I ask, flexing my hips into her again without thinking. I can't help but act on instinct right now. And my body is telling me that I have to get inside this woman as fast as fucking possible.

"Would you believe it if I told you that I'd already thought about this?" she says, and I jerk my head back to meet her eyes.

"When?" I ask, watching her closely.

"Tonight, actually," she says, and I wait for her to continue. "Kelsey is as Sigma Nu tonight and she saw your team beat the shit out of Sky."

I smile widely, loving that he got what was coming to him, but still wishing I'd delivered the blow myself.

"He deserved it," I say.

"Yeah, well, when I asked if you were there, she went on about how *'bad you have it for me'*, and it just got me thinking." She shrugs her shoulders.

"And what exactly were you thinking?"

She bites her bottom lip and peers up at me. The image of innocence. But I know better.

"About what it would be like with you," she whispers.

"And?" I ask, dying to know her answer.

"I think I'd rather you show me," she says, and my cock twitches between us.

"Jesus," I hiss, burying my nose in the crook of her neck again.

"Didn't you come here to scare me?" she asks, and I lift my head to look at her.

She lowers her lids and looks at me in a way I never thought she would.

I nod my head in answer.

"So," she says, and fists the front of my jacket, tugging me until my chest is pressed tightly to hers. "Make me scream."

CHAPTER 7
RAVEN

His eyes darken with desire, and I pull him down to me, pressing my lips to his. I don't know what I expected it to be like kissing him for the first time, but it wasn't this.

His tongue lashes out at mine in violent sweeps, like he's trying to consume all of me at once. His hand tightens around my throat again, and I smile against his lips.

"Like that, do you?" his gravelly voice ghosts over my face.

"Are you surprised?" I ask, not denying it.

Sky would have never touched me like this, and I've been craving this kind of connection for so long. Someone who knows what they're doing, and how they want to please me without needing any instructions.

"Fuck, no," he chuckles, tightening his grip a little more. "You're a little freak."

His tongue darts out, flicking over my mouth again, and I arch up into him, needing to feel him against me.

"See," he says, arching his brow. "I don't know anyone else who actually enjoys being scared."

"I did not enjoy you scaring the shit out of me, thank you," I quip, my head starting to swim from the lack of blood flow.

"Maybe not in the moment, but looking back… your heart was racing. The exhilaration of running from me, not sure if I'd catch you, had you reeling," he says, and honestly, if I take out the fact that I didn't know it was him at the time, then it was all exciting in a way.

"Okay, but had I known it was you…"

"You wouldn't have fought as hard," he says, and he's right.

He loosens his grip and slides his hand down the column of my throat. "I can still feel the nervous energy buzzing on your skin."

His thumb rubs small circles over my neck, and I break out in chills.

"Fuck, I bet…" he says, but suddenly cuts himself off, shaking his head as he sucks his lip into his mouth.

I watch the motion, completely entranced.

"Bet what?" I ask.

His eyes lift to mine, dark and hungry. My stomach squeezes, and I tighten my legs against his hips.

"I bet your pussy is fucking soaked from it," he practically growls, and my sex clenches in response. "All needy, and wet, and wanting. I can fucking smell it on you."

He draws in a deep breath and groans as he exhales.

He's not wrong. I'm aching to be touched. Dying to be filled by him.

I never thought I'd see this side of Griff, but now that I have, I don't ever want to go back. I can't believe it took me this long to see how badly he wanted me. To see how fucking perfect we'd be together. I was blinded by pure stupidity wrapped in a Sigma Nu polo.

I thought I'd be more hesitant to take this step with Griff, but now I couldn't be more ready. I need him, and I need him right fucking now.

"So fucking wet, Griff. I need you inside me, now," I moan, and watch as lust floods his expression.

"There's no going back after this," he tells me, and I shake my head in response. "No changing your mind and running back to that asshole."

"I won't, I don't want him," I swear, shaking my head faster, curling my fingers tighter into the front of his jacket.

"If we do this, you're fucking mine," he says so possessively that I feel it down to my soul. I've never wanted something more than I want to belong to Griff in this very moment.

"Yours. Only yours," I say, leaning up to capture his lips in mine.

It's a quick peck, really, because he pulls away and

smiles down at me triumphantly. "It's about fucking time."

My lips tug at the corners until I'm grinning just as broadly as Griff. We laugh softly, the excitement of the moment too great to suppress. But then he's dipping his head low and claiming my mouth in a whole new way. He puts every single bit of him behind the kiss, gripping my jaw in one hand while the other drops to my ass. He squeezes hard, tugging me up into him as he rolls his hips into me.

I pull at his jacket trying to remove it, and Griff breaks the kiss long enough to sit up on his knees and tug it and his shirt off over his head, dropping them both to the floor.

"As much as I love you in my clothes, this has to go," he says, fingering the hem of his hoodie.

I sit up and let him help me pull it off. I toss my shirt to the side along with his and look up into his eyes as he stares down at my bare chest.

"Fuck me," he murmurs to himself.

Arching a brow coyly, I say, "That's the plan."

He reaches out and cups my breasts, rolling my nipples between his fingers, his fingertips sliding over my piercings before pinching down hard enough to make me hiss.

He leans forward until I fall back against the bed, staring up at him.

"You can fuck me later, because right now, little Raven, I'm going to ruin you for any other man."

I stare at him curiously before he laughs.

"Who am I kidding? There won't be any other men. It'll just give me goals to beat every time I bury myself in this sweet cunt."

His words are so filthy, they're making me wetter by the second.

He takes my nipple into his mouth, sucking hard before releasing it with a loud pop. He leaves hot, wet, bite marks down my chest and stomach, that quickly cools in the cold night air.

He wastes no time pulling my leggings and panties off, throwing them out of his way. He slides back off the bed, kicks off his boots, and removes the rest of his clothes.

And holy fuck, what a glorious sight he is.

His hard cock juts out away from his body, pointing right at me. He grips it roughly in his hand and pumps the length of it twice while he watches me.

He has to be at least nine inches long. Nearly twice the length of what I've been getting.

He really is going to ruin me, I think.

I drop my knees apart, putting myself on display for him. His eyes zero in on my wet pussy and he looks like he might actually fall to his knees and worship it right here and now.

"You can eat it later," I tell him, reaching up and pinching my nipples. "Right now, I need you to fuck me."

"Deal," he says before stepping forward and wrapping his hands around my ankles. When he lifts them up off the bed, I lift my head to ask him what he's doing, but then I feel myself being spread open, wider and wider. My pussy is gaping, and he's staring down at it with the most restrained will power I've ever witnessed.

"You still on the pill?" he asks, eyes never leaving my pussy.

"Yes," I breathe, mesmerized by the way he watches me.

"Good," he says.

Then, without any pretense, he leans his head forward and spits. I feel it drip down over my clit and run down the center of me, coating everything. An involuntary spasm clenches my sex, and my jaw hangs open. That was the hottest thing I think I've ever seen him do.

"Better close that mouth, or I'm spitting in there next," he says, dragging the head of his cock through my pussy before lining up.

"I think I'd be okay with that," I say, dazed.

"Good to know," he says, and then enters me in one hard thrust.

I come up off the bed like a woman possessed, clawing at the sheets as he holds himself there, fully seated.

"God damn, you're so fucking tight," he pants, brows pinched as he fights not to move yet. "Did you ever even get fucked?"

"Not properly," I have enough mind to answer.

"Well, then, let me rectify that issue for you," he says before sliding out and thrusting back in, holding my knees open as far as they'll go.

The insides of my thighs burn as he drives into me, over and over, hitting so deep that I swear for a minute that I can't breathe.

"This pussy was fucking made for me," he says. "Look at how good you take me."

I lift my head and watch as his cock pumps in and out of me, slick with my arousal. I watch as he releases another trail of spit. It drips down on to my clit, and the sensation is enough to make my head swim.

"Oh fuck, Griffin," I moan his name and he picks up pace.

He releases my knees and drops forward, bracing himself on his left hand near my head while the other hand circles back around my throat. His fingertips press deliciously into my pulse points, holding me in place while he fucks into me so hard, I see stars.

"Griffin... Griffin, oh fuck," I cry out.

Then he rolls his hips, grinding into my pussy with every thrust, and the sensation against my clit has me coming.

The orgasm rips through me. Pulse after pulse until I'm quivering beneath him. He releases his hold on my throat and the rush of blood has me coming a second time. It's completely euphoric.

I reach for his head and pull him down to me, biting

his lower lip and tugging. He groans loudly and thrusts harder until finally his movements become jerky and he stills, coming so hard I can feel it inside of me.

He collapses on top of me for a brief second before rolling to the side. My body feels cold and empty without him, and I shiver.

"You okay?" he asks, his voice all raspy and sexy.

"Fucking amazing," I admit, and he chuckles before I add, "just cold."

He pulls me into his side, kissing my forehead. The heat radiating off him is insane. Now to just find the energy to move beneath the blankets and trap his heat inside.

But he doesn't stay still for long, standing and walking into the bathroom. He brings out a warm washcloth and immediately tends to the mess between my legs, being careful of my sensitive skin.

When he's done, I expect him to come back to bed. Instead, he turns to leave the room.

"Wait, where are you going?" I ask, feeling panicked. He wouldn't seriously just fuck me better than anyone has in my entire life and then leave. I'd like to think I know him better than that.

"To lock up and switch the electricity back on. It's gonna get fucking cold tonight," he says.

"Oh, okay," I say, breathing a sigh of relief.

The corner of his mouth lifts in a sideways grin before he turns and walks back over to me.

"You aren't getting rid of me that easy, little Rave girl," he smiles, and leans down to kiss my lips.

I watch his perfect ass as he exits my room and get an idea.

CHAPTER 8

GRIFFIN

I'm on cloud fucking nine as I make my way down the stairs to lock the doors.

I didn't fully expect tonight to end up like this, but I'm beyond happy that it did. Raven needs someone who pays attention to her and knows what she needs before even she does. She wasn't even getting mediocre treatment with Skylar, and she's the kind of girl who deserves to be fucking worshiped. Something I plan on doing every day for the rest of forever.

Because that's what I see when I look at Raven; forever. There isn't a damn thing I won't do for her, and I'll spend every day making sure she knows how much I love her. Because I do. I have since the first day I saw her freshman year.

I wasn't going to mess this up. Not on my life.

I lock the front door and then make my way to the back. I lock that one and then turn to the laundry room where the breaker box sits nestled into the wall. I flip the main breaker to the house, and all the lights come back on with a loud buzz.

After that, I make my way around the ground floor, switching off lights and the TV. I blow out the candle in the corner and then head back up.

I'm going to have to go into town tomorrow and figure out what I need to fix her door. I honestly hadn't planned on busting it in, but I wasn't lying when I told her I was a little more than determined to get inside to her.

When I approach the door, I notice a soft glow spilling out from the crack in the door. Probably her bedside lamp.

I push the door open and stop.

My mind stalls and then kicks into overdrive at the sight.

Raven, kneeling on the ground before me, hand between her legs. Her fingers are slowly circling her clit, and the salacious look in her eyes has my cock growing hard again.

"What's all this?" I ask, approaching her.

Her eyes zero in on my cock, and her tongue darts out to wet her lips like she can't wait to get a taste.

"I'm not finished with you yet," she says, peering up at me from beneath her dark lashes.

"Oh, no?" I ask, brows raised.

"Not even close," she says, reaching out and placing

her hands on my thighs. They slide higher until she's bracing herself against my hips.

"Well, then, don't let me stop you," I say, and watch as she reaches for my cock. Her small hand circles around my length, and she strokes it much more gently than I touch myself.

I give her a few minutes to touch and explore before reaching down and covering her hand with mine.

"Like this," I tell her, tightening her grip and helping her find a good rhythm for me.

When I think she has it figured out, I release her hand and let her take control. Watching her work my cock is about the hottest fucking thing I've seen. That is, until she parts her plump little lips and pokes her tongue out for a taste.

She licks up the bead of precum on my head and swallows it down before coming back for another taste.

Her mouth opens wider, taking about half of my cock inside. Her warm, wet tongue glides against the bottom of my shaft, and my balls draw up tight to my body, the sensation and the realization that this is the girl I've been dreaming of being with for years is enough to make me blow right now.

I concentrate on holding off a little while longer, watching her head bob up and down as she sucks my cock. When I bump the back of her throat, the moan that escapes me echoes off the walls.

Her eyes glitter in delight, and I reach down, cupping

her beautiful face with a smile. I sweep my thumb over her cheekbone before brushing her hair back and gathering it securely in my hand.

After a few more minutes, she's popping her mouth off me to catch her breath.

"Tired?" I ask, chuckling.

"Nope," she grins back.

"Do you trust me?" I ask, ready to amp this up a couple of notches.

"Always," she says, still panting.

"Good. Open your mouth... wide."

She does as I ask with zero hesitation, opening her mouth wide and peering up at me expectantly.

My dirty little freak.

Seeing her mouth hanging open like that, I can't help but remember what I told her earlier. I reach forward, gripping her jaw in my hand, and bend until my face is hovering inches above hers. Without warning, I spit into her mouth, watching it hit her pink tongue, and then I devour her mouth in a punishing kiss.

Her moans are trapped within the kiss until I pull back and right myself. Her expression is slightly dazed as I reach out and capture her head in my hands.

"Hold on," I tell her as I slide my cock across her tongue and down her throat, not stopping until her pouty little lips kiss the base.

Her hands grip my hips in a panic when she realizes her air supply is cut off.

"Stay calm," I tell her, watching her eyes start to water.

She relaxes, and after a few more seconds, I pull back. She breathes deeply through her nose, but after a few breaths, I pull her back onto my cock, sliding down her tight throat.

"Play with your pussy," I tell her.

I watch her reach between her legs, circling her clit.

"Are you wet for me?" I ask, wiping the tears that spill from her eyes.

She tries to nod, but I'm holding her in place, so the movement is restrained. I slide out again, letting her breathe, watching her fingers move faster and faster.

I grip her head in my hands again and look down at her.

"If this gets to be too much, you tap out, okay?" I tell her, miming a tapping motion against my hip.

She nods in understanding, and I thrust forward, fucking her sweet mouth. Her fingers never let up as I piston forward, sliding over her tongue until my balls draw up tight.

Her eyes meet mine as she pulls her hand from between her leg and reaches up to cradle my balls in her hand.

"Ah, fuck," I say, and she sticks out her tongue as far as she can while I thrust forward, coming hard down her throat.

She stays there, unmoving, until I've given her every last drop. I release her face and pull back, keeping my eyes fixed on hers. When she closes her mouth and swallows, I almost nut again.

"You're fucking perfect," I tell her, grabbing her hand and helping her to her feet.

I bend and cover her mouth with mine, dragging my tongue across hers as I bury my hands in her hair.

Walking us backwards, I pull her down on top of me, never breaking the connection. I could do this for the rest of my life and never get tired of it.

She shifts her body until she is straddling me. Her wet pussy kisses my cock and I jerk up against her.

Her moans spill out between our lips and she drops down to grind against me harder.

"Holy shit," I curse, still sensitive from my orgasm.

"It'll just take me a minute," she says, rolling her hips forward. Her pussy drags against my cock again, and I twitch.

I grab her hips to stop her movements and she looks down at me questioningly.

"It's sensitive right now. But, let me help you," I offer and she's quick to wave away my offer.

"You don't have to, that's fine," she says, trying to climb off me.

I furrow my brows and hold her in place. "It's not fine; you should get yours, too. There's nothing wrong with that."

"Yeah, but—"

"No buts," I tell her, and then swat her ass. "Except

maybe this one."

I waggle my brows at her suggestively and she laughs. "You really don't have to."

"I know that. But I want to," I tell her in all seriousness. "Plus, I do recall you saying I could eat this pussy later."

She stills and looks down at me, concern in her eyes. She looks like a completely different woman from the one choking on my cock two minutes ago. What the fuck did that asshole do to make her so unsure of herself?

"You still want to? Even after we…" she asks, trailing off toward the end.

"Fuck yeah. You really think that's going to stop me?" I ask, looking up at her like she's the crazy person, not me.

When she shrugs, looking unsure, I look up at her, adopting a more serious tone.

"Any man who won't eat a pussy that he just thoroughly fucked isn't a man you want hanging around," I tell her matter-of-factly.

She rolls her eyes playfully as if to say, *'no shit'*, and I swat her ass again.

"Now, climb up here and let me eat my pussy."

CHAPTER 9
RAVEN

Griff urges me forward until I'm straddling his face. I hover there for a second. This is new territory for me.

Sky would never have been into this. Hell, he never would have gotten past his first orgasm, and I would have been left to take care of myself in the bathroom via showerhead.

I may still have a use for it if I can get Griff in there with me, fucking me from behind.

"Sit," he tells me, and I lower myself a fraction of an inch.

He arches his brow at me, not amused.

"Woman, when I say sit, I mean fucking suffocate me with your pussy. If I die, then at least I'll die happy."

I chuckle at his absurdity, but it's cut short when he reaches up, grabbing my hips, and pulls me down until I'm fully seated on his mouth.

Reaching out, I brace myself on my headboard, ready

to lift off at a moment's notice. But when he opens his mouth, and the first swipe of his tongue slides over my pussy, my head falls back, and I cry out in pleasure.

He grips my ass cheeks in his hands and spreads me open wider before sinking his tongue deep inside of me. He pulls out and drags the tip between my lips until he finds my clit and circles it.

I grind down against his mouth and he moans in approval, sucking hard at my lips, kissing my cunt like it's his fucking job. When he goes back to thrusting his tongue inside of me, fucking me with that sinful mouth of his, my legs begin to shake.

I'm so close, teetering on the edge.

He moves one of his hands closer, sliding a finger inside of me while he bites down on my clit. I jerk against his mouth and take my breasts in my hands, tweaking my nipples as he finger-fucks me.

"I'm so fucking close, Griff," I cry out, rolling my hips against him.

He removes his finger, quickly replacing it with his tongue, and slides it back to my ass, pushing slightly against my hole.

"Oh fuck," I cry out, riding his face harder now.

His tongue slides in and out of my pussy relentlessly while he works his finger against my ass, until finally he slips in.

Stars explode behind my eyes with the most delicious pleasure as he works both of my holes until I'm screaming his name.

I come hard, reaching down between my legs and sinking my fingers into his hair, holding him in place until the last waves of pleasure wash over my body.

My legs are jelly when I try to climb off, and Griff has to help me steady myself. He pulls the blankets back and helps me crawl beneath them before sliding in beside me.

He holds me close while my breathing evens out, and then after a few minutes, when my heart rate returns to normal, he speaks.

"Are you okay?" His voice is gentle and soothing as he strokes my hair back from my face.

"Mmm," I hum in answer, and he chuckles.

"I wasn't sure if you'd ever done anything like that before. We never really made it a habit to talk about our sex lives," he says.

"Well, there wasn't really much to talk about as far as mine went," I tell him, scoffing.

"Yeah, I didn't figure," he chuckles and draws me close.

"Not that I didn't love ever fucking second of that," he starts, and I lift my gaze to meet his. "But I have to ask. Are you okay with all of that? I know my tastes can be a little out there for some, so just know that you don't ever have to do anything you don't like."

As if I couldn't love this guy anymore.

"Honestly, a lot of that was new to me. But I loved it," I say truthfully. "As long as it's with you, there isn't much I don't think I wouldn't try."

"Careful, that's a dangerous thing to say to me. I've already got about ten different positions I want to get you into," he laughs, but I can see the seriousness in his eyes.

"Okay, but maybe tomorrow," I say playfully. "After that last orgasm, I think I may fall into a coma."

"You know," he says, looking toward the ceiling as if in thought, "somnophilia is definitely something I could get behind, especially with you."

I swat at his chest, and he captures my hand, kissing my fingertips. I draw my lip between my teeth and decide to keep how much that turned me on to myself. At least for now.

Being fucked in my sleep honestly sounds pretty fucking amazing. Especially if it's with Griffin.

I curl into his side, resting my head on his chest.

This Halloween started out like shit but leave it to my best friend — we're going to have to amend that title — to completely save the day and make this one of the best and most memorable Halloweens yet.

I can't wait for next year.

CHAPTER 10
GRIFFIN

I'm woken up early the next morning by Coco kneading her little paws into my chest. The sun has just barely risen, but when I recall Raven having locked the cat door, I throw back the covers and slide out of bed.

"Alright, alright, let's go outside," I say to the little fluff ball as she weaves in between my feet.

I step into my jeans and reach for the hoodie Raven was wearing last night, pulling it over my head as I follow Coco downstairs.

She darts outside the second I open the back door. I follow her out onto the back steps, taking in the mess from last night.

"Shit," I sigh, rubbing the back of my neck. I forgot about that.

It isn't quite as much as it looked like last night, and I trudge down the steps, picking up the trash as I go. Raven shouldn't have to do it, even if it was an accident. I knocked it over.

By the time I'm finished and have the trash can tucked back securely against the house, I meet Coco at the back door and we both head inside.

It's way too early to be awake right now, but I know that if this cat doesn't get fed immediately, she'll never leave us alone. So, I pull out a can of food and deposit it in her food dish before scratching her behind the ears and heading back upstairs.

Raven is in exactly the same position as when I left, which isn't a surprise to me at all. She can sleep through anything. No joke.

During a group movie night at my place, she'd fallen asleep on the couch, and even after the movie ended and people started turning on lights and getting up to stretch or go to the bathroom, she never stirred. Skylar had thought it would be funny to try to stack shit on her forehead, but I shut that down real quick. I can't stand people who get entertained at someone else's expense.

Still, she didn't wake up for hours. Nearly everyone had left except Skylar, Kelsey, and Rave.

"I'm not staying here all night," Skylar sighs dramatically.

"No one said you had to," I say, glaring at him from across the room.

"Oh, you'd just love that, wouldn't you?" he sneers. He knows how much I like her. That shit is obvious to other guys, and he just loves that he beat me to her. He also knows that I'm gonna be right here waiting the second his dumbass fucks up.

"Yeah, the sooner you're out of my house, the better. The

only reason you're even here right now is because of Raven," I tell him, wishing I could just pick him up and toss him out on his ass. I don't think that'd go over so well with my best friend, though.

We sit there in silence for another few minutes before he stands up. "Fuck it, I'm trying again." He says and leans over to try to shake her awake.

When she doesn't wake up, Kelsey and I chuckle, rolling our eyes at how dumb this guy is.

"Seriously, I'm not sleeping here," he says again, and I'm about done with his fucking bitching.

Thankfully, Kelsey steps in before I have a chance to stand up from my position on the couch and get in his face about it.

"Jesus, Skylar, I'll stay with her and make sure she gets home tomorrow," she tells him.

I expect him to fight her on this the same way he would me, but he doesn't.

"Really?" he asks her, his eyebrows arching in surprise... or maybe relief. I can't tell.

"Really. Go," she waves him away.

He grins enthusiastically, pulling out his phone and heading toward the door, likely before Kelsey can change her mind.

When he's finally gone, I look over to Kelsey and see that she's suspicious of the very thing I am.

"Who do you think he was texting?" she asks.

"Not my business. But if he's dumb enough to fuck around on Rae, then I'll have no problems beating his ass for it," I shrug.

"Yeah, because that would really tear you up inside," she says sarcastically, laughing through a yawn.

"You can go home, you know. You don't have to stay; I'll get her home tomorrow," I say, nodding toward Raven where she sleeps on the couch.

"Oh, I know. I'm going home to sleep in my own bed. No offense, but I'm not about to try to sleep on this thing," she says, throwing her thumb over her shoulder toward the unoccupied loveseat.

"None taken," I laugh.

It's a matter of minutes before Kelsey has gathered all of her things and headed out, locking the door behind her and leaving me and Rave alone.

Sure, we've been alone together plenty of times, but with the lights in the living room dimmed, and the house all quiet with the promise of sleep right around the corner, it feels different. Almost forbidden.

Fuck that, though. She's always belonged to me. Nothing about her is forbidden. Not to me. Not forever.

I stand from my recliner and go around the room, shutting off all the lights, before going over to Raven and scooping her up against my chest. There is no way in hell I'm leaving her down here on the couch by herself. She'll be sore as hell in the morning. But also, I don't know when I'll get this opportunity again, so I'm not wasting it.

I carry her upstairs to my room and lay her down at the foot of my bed. Bending down, I quickly remove her shoes and set them near the wall. I contemplate for a moment just how far

*I should undress her and then say '*fuck it*' and reach for the button on her jeans.*

If anything, I can just feign innocence. It's not like I haven't been doing that for the last year and a half, anyway. Every single time she caught me staring at her, and I'd tell her that I was just spacing out, when really I was picturing all the different ways I wanted to fuck her.

I pop the button on her jeans and hook my fingers inside the waist, peeling them down over her hips and down her legs before dropping them to the floor.

She's in the tiniest little black thong, and my cock instantly grows hard. Her skin looks smooth to the touch, but I keep my hands at my sides. If I let myself touch her, there's no guarantee that I'll be able to stop myself.

After standing there for a solid minute, taking her in, I reach for the hem of her shirt and start pushing it up her torso. Might as well, right? If I'm going to make sure she's comfortable and all,

I lift her into a sitting position and remove her top, throwing it behind me with her pants.

When I take her in, I bite my bottom lip in some kind of attempt to control myself.

I've never been so pleased with a woman's hatred toward bras, because Raven almost never wears one. But with perky little tits like hers, why even bother? The metal glint of her barbells catches the light and I imagine biting down on her nipples and tugging at them until she's crying out my name.

"Fucking hell," I hiss, staring down at the most perfect,

beautiful, mouthwatering woman I have ever known, nothing but a scrap of material covering her little pussy, and all I can think about is burying my cock deep inside of her.

Shit, I could probably get away with it, too. She probably wouldn't even wake up.

I shake my head, erasing the thought from my mind. Despite the current situation, trust and respect are actually a pretty big thing for me. I won't touch her without her consent. Looking on the other hand… that's a bit of a gray area for me. See, she'll know I saw her mostly naked when she wakes up in my clothes in the morning. What I do while she's mostly naked is not something she needs to worry about right now.

With my mind made up, I yank my shirt up over my head and strip out of my jeans.

Standing naked before her, watching her tits rise and fall with every shallow breath she takes, I take my cock in my hand and pump it. Precum glistens at the tip, and I rub my thumb over it, using it as lube. But it isn't enough.

Before I go any further, I reach out and nudge the insides of her knees until her legs part just enough for me to see her barely contained pussy nestled between her legs.

Spitting into my palm, I wrap my hand around my length and start stroking. Several times, I'm tempted to hook a finger inside her panties and shift them out of the way for a better view, but I know that if I get any closer to her, I'm gonna drop to my knees and eat her sweet cunt until her honey is running down my face.

The mental image is exactly the fuel I need, and before I

know it, I'm coming hard into my hand. I'm practically shaking after that release, and I stand there for a minute to catch my breath.

The urge to reach inside her panties and coat her in my cum is strong, but I tell myself to shelve that idea for the future, and turn toward the bathroom to clean up.

Once I'm done, I pull on a pair of gym shorts and grab a second pair for Rave, as well as one of my shirts. It's going to swallow her given her small frame, but that just makes it even better.

I get her dressed again and position her higher up on the bed, pulling the covers in around her. It takes me an extra five minutes to calm myself down before I'm able to crawl in beside her.

I don't think I slept at all that night. Not with the temptation of having her so close to me there all night.

Surprisingly, she wasn't even concerned with the fact that I changed her into my clothes, which instantly had my mind concocting reasons to need to do it again.

As I stand at the foot of her bed and watch her now, all the things I wanted to do to her that night flood my mind.

And this time, there's nothing stopping me from having her exactly how I want her.

After I toss my clothes back on the floor, I pull the blanket down her body, slowly, uncovering inch by inch until she's exposed to me.

She's laying on her stomach with her juicy ass on

display. Her pretty little pussy tucked away between her thighs, just barely peeking out.

I crawl up over her legs, stopping just above her ass. The angle is a bit awkward, so I reach up and grab a pillow, folding it over and sliding it beneath her hips. Her ass is now at the perfect angle, and I reach out, taking her cheeks in my hands, squeezing them until the barest glimpse of her asshole is visible.

Leaning closer, I spread her farther apart and swipe my tongue over her tight hole, rimming her slowly, wondering if she'll still get off even if she's asleep. If not, I'll eat her pussy until she screams once she's awake.

I probe the tip of my tongue just past the tight ring of muscles, dying to get inside. I won't take her ass while she's asleep, though. Not completely anyway. I want her awake for that experience. But I can't pass up the opportunity to play with it just a little.

Pulling back, I stretch her until her ass opens up just the tiniest bit, and I spit a slow stream of saliva into her hole. I release one cheek and use my middle finger to rub it in before pressing against her ass and watching my finger slide in.

My cock is leaking against her sheets as I twist my finger from side to side, two knuckles deep in her sweet ass. I manage to slide it all the way in, fucking entranced by the sight.

I'm going to love fucking her here, I can already tell.

I pull my finger out and suck it clean before leaning

forward and slipping my tongue over her again.

Her pussy is wet, which answers my previous question. I spread her legs and drop my head down, sliding my tongue over her clit and dipping inside her to lap up all her sweetness. The taste is fucking maddening, and I can't hold back any longer.

Getting into position, I coat her with my cum before thrusting inside. I fill her in one swift movement, throwing my head back as the sensation of her warmth squeezes me. I don't hesitate this time, pulling back and slamming back in, fucking into her with everything I have.

She shifts higher on the bed, and I stop just long enough to drag her back down, away from the risk of hitting her head against the headboard.

I grip her hips in my hands and pump into her until I feel the edges of my orgasm creeping up. Slipping my hand between Raven and the pillow, I circle her clit, just to be safe, and when her pussy spasms around my cock, I let go, coming hard. I pull out and make sure to coat her asshole in it, too. Just because.

When I fall down beside her, I'm seriously surprised that she didn't wake up through all of that. She really does sleep like the dead.

I hook an arm around her middle and drag her back into my body, sliding my semi-hard cock between her ass cheeks and passing the fuck out.

EPILOGUE
RAVEN

Griffin and I spent the entire weekend having sex, and even though I can still feel him inside of me with every step I take, I have zero complaints.

I'd woken up the morning after Halloween in his arms, cum still wet between my legs.

When I'd asked him how it had gotten there, he didn't even flinch. Just told me that after I'd made the comment about being fucked into a coma after the crazy good sex that first night, it got his mind spinning. He'd admitted to having fantasies about fucking me in my sleep, and even admitted to jacking off to my naked body the night I slept at his house back in spring. I was only momentarily shocked, but it quickly faded. I honestly find the idea to be pretty fucking hot. And apparently, I even get off in my sleep, so there's that.

It's Monday morning, and as much as we didn't want to, we had classes to get back to.

Still, that didn't stop Griff from pressing me to my front door this morning, pulling down my pants, and coming in my panties before pulling them back up into place.

"I want you to remember whose pussy this is when you're wondering around campus today," he's said with a devious glint in his eyes.

We almost didn't make it out the door on time. Not that I would have complained about another whole day in with Griff.

I'm just cutting through the quad when someone grabs me by the shoulder, spinning me around.

"What the fuck?" I shout, reaching up to cradle my shoulder.

"Baby, I've been trying to get a hold of you all weekend," Skylar says in his typical whiny voice.

He looks like hell. His eyebrow and lip are split, his nose probably broken, and his eyes are black. I can only imagine what the rest of him looks like. I almost feel bad for him, but then the momentary lapse in judgment passes and I step back.

"Well, I don't know why, considering we broke up and aren't together anymore," I roll my eyes and go to turn away, but his fucking hand grabs for my shoulder again.

"Unless you want to lose the fingers, I'd take your fucking hand off me," I tell him, knowing that Griff is going to meet me out here any second.

I don't really give a shit about what happened to Skylar, but I don't want Griffin getting into any trouble.

"Look, I fucked up. I know I did. I'm sorry, it won't happen again," he starts rambling, and I hold my hand up to stop him.

"Skylar, I honestly couldn't even care. Fuck whoever you want, it doesn't matter to me," I tell him.

His expression is unsure as he watches me.

"Really? You don't mind?"

Fucking dumbass.

"Why would I? You're not my problem anymore?" I tell him, shrugging my shoulders.

I catch sight of Griffin exiting the building next to us, and his expression instantly shifts.

"Now, since I don't have anything else to say to you, I suggest you leave before my boyfriend gets overhear," I smile, scrunching my nose in a 'fuck you' fashion before turning around and walking toward Griffin.

"What the fuck did he want?" he asks, his disdain for Skylar still very real.

"Oh, you know. He's sorry, it'll never happen again, blah blah blah, I don't care," I say, rolling my eyes before stepping into my man's embrace and wrapping my arms around his neck.

"What a dumbass," he shakes his head.

"Clearly," I smile up at him and his stoney expression dissolves away, the corners of his lips twitching as he looks down at me.

"Are you still wearing my cum?" he asks, and my stomach flutters to life.

"Yes, but most of it has soaked into my panties," I tell him. "I have twenty minutes until my next class, though. You want to sneak into one of the empty classrooms and fuck me over the professor's desk?" I wiggle my eyebrows up at him and he chuckles, low and devious.

He dips his head to my throat and bites softly beneath my ear. "I thought you'd never ask."

He takes me by the hand and leads me back inside the building.

Last week, I would have told anyone who asked that it was the worst Halloween of my life. But ask me now, and I'll tell you that it's been the most exhilarating time of my life.

It's also the start of a brand-new tradition for me and Griff. But next year, when he breaks into my house, he promised to let me try to fight him off before he takes me 'against my will'.

I can't fucking wait.

*Continue reading for a glimpse
of what happened to the boyfriend who found
Skylar and Kiersten in the library.*

CHAPTER 1
SHANE

The flickering glow of the jack-o'-lantern on my doorstep casts eerie shadows across the room. It's Halloween night, and I'm stuck here, alone, with nothing but mind-numbing silence, and the scene from that day burned into my mind.

I caught my girlfriend cheating.

Ex-girlfriend, I remind myself.

I sink into the worn-out couch, the echoes of laughter and excited chatter from people outside, making their way to the party at Sigma Nu, a stark contrast to the irritation I feel.

She and I had planned on going to the party together, but that all changed really fast. I'd rather sit here alone than go and have to witness her hanging all over that douchebag, Skylar.

The glow of my phone pierces through the dimness of the room. Every buzz and ding grating on my nerves.

Each notification a twisted mix of annoyance and morbid curiosity.

I've done my best to ignore them as they trickle in, but after the sixth one in a row, I give in and click on the text thread from my roommates.

> Dude ur missing out! This shit is crazy

> He's right. There's plenty of chicks here to distract yourself with.

> Are u ignoring us?

> I think he's ignoring us, bro 🙄

> Really? What gave it away?

> Holy fuck, man!! Check this shit out!

A video message comes through next. My thumb hovers over the play button, hesitant to watch. Tristan is the kind of dumbass that would find it funny to send me a video catching Kiersten in the act. I really don't want to see that.

But then another text from Connor comes in, leaving me even more curious.

> Fuck man, I missed it!!

I click play and draw my phone closer. Loud shouts and muffled screams blare through the speakers, filling the otherwise silent room. Music bumps heavily in the background as people crowd around. It takes a second or two before I get a clear shot of what's happening. When I do, the corners of my lips twitch into a satisfied grin.

A group of guys circle Skylar, beating the shit out of him. Not enough to send the guy to the hospital or anything, but it was definitely enough to send him a message. I just wish I knew who it was from.

> What was that about?

HE SPEAKS!!

I just talked to Mason and Kyson Graves from the lacrosse team. They said they're Captain, Griffin Abbott, orchestrated the whole thing.

> Griffin did? Why?

U know that dude is crazy lol

I guess Skylar's ex is his best friend.

Yes sure, 'best friend' 😏 lol

> **Makes sense**

U should come out!

> **Nah, I'm good. I'll see you guys tomorrow** 😈

I close out of the messaging app and drop my phone to the couch beside me, a twisted sense of justice settling over me.

Initially, I hadn't even been pissed at the guy. It wasn't his fault that she decided to cheat on me. But after finding out that he knew that Kiersten and I were together, and he was cheating on his girlfriend, I couldn't stand him.

What kind of asshole does shit like that?

Skylar Smith, apparently.

It had been last week. I left my notebook in the library after study group and ran back to grab it. One of my buddies on the football team said he'd just seen Kiersten a few minutes ago heading toward the shelves in the back. Thinking that maybe she'd been looking for me, I grabbed my notebook and headed in that direction.

Part of me wishes I hadn't, but honestly, I'm glad I did.

I hear the sounds before I see her, and I know.

She has her jean skirt flipped up over her ass, thong

pulled to the side while Skylar fucks her from behind. His uncoordinated thrusts slapping off her ass as she covers her mouth with her hands to muffle her moans.

I stand there for a good minute, as the shock fades, and then lean up against the shelf, crossing my arms over my chest before clearing my throat.

"Wow, you're really giving it to her, huh?" I say.

Their heads whip in my direction and Kiersten stands abruptly, simultaneously breaking their connection. Skylar quickly shoves his micro-dick back inside his pants, and Kiersten pushes her skirt back into place before turning to face me.

"Don't look at me like that, Shane," she sighs, placing her hands on her hips. "I mean, you can't honestly tell me you're surprised."

"That my girlfriend had the nerve to cheat on me? Yeah, I'd say I'm a little surprised. Though, I feel like I shouldn't be," I tell her.

"What is that supposed to mean?" she hisses under her breath.

"Ever since we lost the state championship last year, you've been acting different. Distancing yourself. Are you really that shallow?" I ask her.

"I am not shallow. I just can't be with some football loser anymore," she says, backing up and placing her hand on Skylar's chest. "I'm with a real man now. We're done."

I scoff, rolling my eyes. "Oh, no, say it isn't so. What

am I ever going to do without you?"

Her jaw falls open, and she looks at me like I just spit in her face.

"Hope you like vanilla, man. That's about all you're in for," I say, nodding my head at Skylar.

Was that uncalled for? Probably, but it felt good in the moment.

I pat the shelf beside me twice and turn to walk away.

That was a little over a week ago, and the pitying looks I've received since then are starting to grow annoying. I'm really not that broken up over it; things haven't been the same in months, and I knew that an end was inevitable. I just didn't expect her to cheat and then call me a loser.

Honestly, did she realize who she chose to cheat on me with? Talk about a loser. I felt bad for whoever he'd been dating. Word is she didn't find out until someone blasted it all over the university blog. That had to suck.

With nothing better to do, I pick up my laptop and open Netflix. I scroll for about five minutes, looking for something to watch and settling on some random horror movie.

I'm just about to hit play when my doorbell rings.

"Who the fuck?" I say, muttering to myself as I crane my head around to view the front door.

People here don't trick-or-treat, but I wouldn't put it past someone drunk off their ass to start ringing people's doorbells.

It's silent for a minute, and I assume whomever it was must have left, but then it chimes again, and I sigh loudly before standing.

CHAPTER 2
ARIA

I stand there, tugging down the front of my dress as I wait, hoping Shane answers the door.

I don't know if you can actually call what I'm wearing a dress; there isn't much to it. The strapless body-con barely even covers my ass. If I bend over, his neighbors are going to get an eyeful.

It's cold tonight, and a chill skitters over my legs. Even with the oversized zip-up hoodie on, I was freezing.

A minute goes by, and no one answers. I don't see any movement inside either. Maybe I shouldn't have come here tonight. I knew that showing up was a huge risk, especially after that insane breakup last week.

I saw the whole thing happen. Well, not all of it, but enough.

We'd just wrapped up with study group and I wanted to check out a few books for an upcoming report, so I hung around.

I didn't really need the study group, but when Shane had leaned forward in class at the beginning of term and asked if I understood any of what was going on, I told him about the group and how I didn't think it would interfere with his football schedule.

He'd wanted to know if I ever went, and in a spur of the moment's decision, I told him I did. I joined the very next day.

For an hour and a half, two nights a week for the last six weeks, I got to spend time with one of the hottest guys on campus. The only problem was, he had a girlfriend. Still, I showed up to every study session, if only just to be around him.

Shane Donnavan has this energy that you can't help but be drawn to. Like a moth to a flame. And damn if I didn't let myself get burned every time. He was fascinating, and I couldn't put my finger on why.

He had layers, that much I could tell.

Smart, and funny, and a gentleman, but also this kickass athlete that charmed everyone around him. Then there was the part that intrigued me the most. The glint in his eyes when he didn't think anyone was watching him. A dark tendril of something that crept out when he was lost in thought.

I'd kill to know what those thoughts were.

What made him look into the empty space before him with so much heat? It was enough to make me shift in my seat whenever I caught him in those moments. More than once I'd left study group wet and on edge, racing back to my dorm room to alleviate the ache building between my legs.

After a few weeks, it was his face I'd start to envision when I'd read my spicey novels. His dark eyes I'd picture watching me as my fingers snuck beneath the hem of my panties.

I wanted him. That much was clear. But it wasn't until last week that I thought maybe, just maybe, I'd have a chance.

The back of my neck tingled, and somehow, I knew he was near. I'd scanned the room and saw him walking back over to the tables we'd all just been sitting at. He bent and grabbed his notebook from the floor and stopped to talk to one of his friends. I watched as he made his way toward the back corner of the library, and curious as I was, I followed.

Keeping at least two rows of shelves between us, I watched as he stumbled upon his girlfriend having sex with some other guy. My stomach dropped, and I was instantly infuriated on his behalf.

How could she cheat on Shane? He's such a great guy.

"Wow, you're really giving it to her, huh?" I heard him say.

I could just make out the sounds of people pulling on their clothes.

"Don't look at me like that, Shane. I mean, you can't honestly tell me you're surprised."

"That my girlfriend had the nerve to cheat on me? Yeah, I'd say I'm a little surprised. Though I feel like I shouldn't be."

Standing up on my tiptoes, I could just barely make out the top of Kiersten's blonde head.

"What is that supposed to mean?" she whisper-yelled at him.

"Ever since we lost the state championship last year, you've been acting different. Distancing yourself. Are you really that shallow?"

"I am not shallow. I just can't be with some football loser anymore. I'm with a real man now. We're done."

I'd just stood there, completely shocked by what she'd said. I wanted to march right over there and punch her in the face. Shane is not a loser, but she sure as hell is a bitch.

"Oh, no, say it isn't so. What am I ever going to do without you? Hope you like vanilla, man. That's about all you're in for."

I'd tried my best not to laugh, but she had it coming.

When Shane didn't show up for study group earlier this week, I grew concerned. I knew he had to be upset, or embarrassed, or something, but I missed seeing him.

Kiersten had shown up, though. Not to our group, but she and her friends formed their own little group two tables away from us.

I caught bits of their conversation here and there, and it quickly became clear that they weren't there to study, but to talk shit.

"Was he mad?" one of her friends asked?

"Oh my God, so mad," Kiersten laughed. It was total bullshit. Nothing I heard the other day would indicate that Shane was more than annoyed. I had no idea how he was feeling now though, so I slid back in my chair, angling my head slightly for a better listen.

"Well, duh. He'd have to be crazy not to be mad over losing you," her other friend preened over her.

"Oh, he's crazy alright," Kiersten scoffed.

"What?"

"Really?"

"Spill, girl."

They were all bitches. I didn't care what anyone else thought; I didn't like them at all.

"Ugh, he was so weird. Like, in the bedroom… he tried to tie me up once," she gasped, and I arched my brows in interest. "He wanted me to let him do butt stuff, too, and I was so not about to let him put it back there."

"So gross," her friends chimed in.

Needless to say, that after that day, my curiosity about Shane grew and grew. He starred in all of my dirty fantasies, and when I imagined him doing to me all the things he'd wanted to do with Kiersten, it left me hot and flustered.

I could give him those things. I wanted to.

Sure, I'm fairly quiet and usually have my nose stuck in a book, but the things I would let that man do to me are endless.

So, here I stand. Skintight scrap of a dress, no bra, no panties, and the brand-new plug I'd purchased yesterday tuck snugly in my ass, the pretty little jewel on the end visible when I bend over, ready to offer myself up on a silver platter.

I just hoped he would be interested, otherwise I'd feel like a complete fool.

Drawing in a deep breath, I reach my hand out and ring the bell again.

DIRTY LITTLE TRICK

ABOUT THE AUTHOR

Avery James King is a writer of Dark Romance, Romantic Suspense, New Adult Romance, and Erotica. She enjoys writing stories with gritty heroes, powerful heroines, and tragic backstories that keep you turning the page.

She lives in Oklahoma with her son, and their dogs. When she isn't writing, she enjoys reading from her favorite authors, binging shows on Netflix, and almost always has a cup of coffee nearby. She also owns and runs a graphic design business, Star Child Designs, that is geared toward helping fellow authors achieve beautiful designs and bookish creations.

You can find Avery on these social platforms:
Instagram
Facebook
X (formerly Twitter)
TikTok
Goodreads
Amazon
Website

Join Avery's reader group Avery James King's Devious Readers for all of the latest updates on upcoming projects.

OTHER BOOKS

THE STREETS OF SANCTE ALTO
THE REBEL PRINCE
THE JADED PRINCESS
FRACTURED ROYALS

WILDWOOD UNIVERSITY
DIRTY LITTLE TRICK
STICKY LITTLE TREAT
WICKED LITTLE TEASE
NAUGHTY LITTLE THRILL

LOVER'S LANE SERIAL NOVELLA SERIES
THE MATCH
THE SETUP

PROJECT LOVE & LINGERIE
PROJECT LOVE & LINGERIE

STANDALONES
THE COUNTDOWN TO YOU
LOVE YOU MORE
KIDNAPPED ON CHRISTMAS
SANTA'S NAUGHTY HELPER

Printed in Great Britain
by Amazon